Checking It Twice

Samantha Wayland

Also by Samantha Wayland

Checking It Twice

Published by Loch Awe Press
P.O. Box 5481
Wayland, MA 01778

ISBN 978-1-940839-13-4

Edited by Meghan Miller
Cover Art by Caitlin Fry

Dedication

For Stephanie—my writing buddy, cheerleader, and fellow hockey nut. I'm pretty sure the last three books wouldn't have happened without you, so this is long overdue.

Acknowledgements

As noted above, a special shout out must go to Stephanie Kay, who has kicked my ass and cheered me on through the last few books. A big thank you also (always) to Victoria Morgan, who sticks by me even when I write about stuff that makes her blush.

A huge round of applause to my spectacular editor, Meghan Miller, who is still putting up with me after all these years. And to Caitlin Fry, who has taken in stride my sudden (and hopefully temporary) need to give all kinds of weird input on my covers. And to Cindy, for being the keenest proofreader I could ever have hoped for!

And lastly, as always, my love and gratitude to my family. Nine books in and they still think this is as fun as I do. How'd I get so lucky?

Chapter One

It was a sad state of affairs when dumping a couple of gallons of lube on some unsuspecting rookie's head no longer gave a man a thrill.

The rest of the guys in the locker room cracked up as the newest Moncton Ice Cat wiped the stream of gunk from his eyes and grinned at all of them. He seemed genuinely pleased with the attention.

It wasn't that Alexei *wasn't* satisfied with his efforts to welcome the new guy—lubrication style—but if someone else volunteered to step up and take over torturing the newbies, Alexei wouldn't object. He had other things he wanted to focus on.

He watched their newest right wing leave a slick trail across the floor on the way to his locker, smiling when Mike stepped aside to let him pass with a wide margin. Mike caught Alexei's eye, and, like always, something tightened in Alexei's chest, squeezing in response to the soft affection in Mike's smile as he quirked an eyebrow.

That. That was what made Alexei happy these days.

Alexei remembered pulling this same prank on Mike when he'd first shown up in Moncton, more than four years ago. Mike hadn't taken it quite as well, though he'd faked it for all he was worth. Alexei had seen through that façade, though. Had seen right into Mike and been drawn to him from the first instant.

A lot had changed since then, but not that. There was never a time Alexei hadn't been drawn to Mike. Falling in love with him had been easy. Admitting it had been a little harder, but done long ago.

With a last lingering look, Mike turned for the showers.

Alexei startled when someone bumped into him from behind.

"You going to clean this up, Belov?" Callum, one of the team's owners, asked with a pointed look at the congealing puddle by the door. Anyone who didn't know Callum would have thought he was pissed. Alexei knew better.

He grinned. "I already paid the cleaning crew double their daily rate. In cash."

"You better have," Callum said sternly, but there was no mistaking the twinkle in his eyes. Eyes that widened with alarm when his husband, Rupert, stepped through the door and directly into the puddle.

The squawking that ensued? Now, *that* was funny.

"Goddamn it, Alexei," Rupert shouted above the laughter echoing through the room.

"It's not my fault you always forget when the new guys are showing up," Alexei said.

Rupert sighed and glared at the men laughing at him. "Laugh it up, guys. I'll trade every last one of you to Newfoundland by the New Year." As the team's manager, he could do it.

Some of the younger players looked alarmed for the ten seconds it took Rupert's frown to crack into a smile. He tried, and failed, to turn a severe look on Alexei. "You're paying to have these shoes cleaned."

"Yes, boss."

Rupert rolled his eyes, gingerly stepping out of the puddle.

"Good game tonight. Congratulations on your third shutout this season," Callum said while he waited for Rupert to shake off his foot—which wasn't helping—and join them.

"Thanks," Alexei said, trying not to rub his hip too obviously. By the look Callum gave him, he wasn't succeeding. "I'm glad we get to go into the holiday break with that game."

Rupert nodded, casting a furtive glance around the room. "Speaking of the holidays, did you—"

"Shhhh..." Alexei hissed quietly.

"I know," Rupert said even more quietly. "But did you—?"

"Yes," Alexei whispered furiously.

"So, tonight?" Callum asked, his eyes lighting up.

Alexei recalled what he had planned for that night and couldn't help his slow smile. "No, not tonight."

Callum and Rupert cast each other amused and slightly alarmed looks. Rupert arched an eyebrow at Alexei. "Now I know why you wanted to know if we'd be out this evening."

Alexei shrugged innocently. He wasn't going to give details—not that Rupert or Callum would ever ask—and he wasn't sure if anything would happen anyway.

"Forget about that. I want to know when you're going to do it," Callum pressed.

Alexei was perfectly aware Callum wasn't referring to his little surprise for Mike that night, but another gift altogether. "I don't know. Not Christmas Eve Eve or whatever tonight is called."

"But Christmas?" Rupert asked, so enthusiastically he sounded as if the gift were for *him*.

Alexei frowned and rubbed his chin thoughtfully. "In Russia, the big holiday for gifts is New Year's Day. Maybe I'll wait until then."

This had the desired impact. Rupert looked like he might die if he had to wait that long. Callum didn't look much better. Alexei could barely hold in his laughter.

"But that's *more than a week away*," Rupert whined.

Alexei did laugh now. "You sound like Oliver."

Rupert's expression made it clear what he thought of the comparison to his five-year-old brother, whom Rupert and Callum were raising.

Before Alexei could tease him further, Callum cleared his throat loudly. And really fucking obviously.

Alexei refused to turn around. He had no doubt Mike was coming out of the shower room. He cast a baleful look at his ridiculous friends and their innocent expressions.

Mike stared into his locker until he was sure he could

contain his grin, then calmly went about the business of getting dressed and ready to head out. If Alexei didn't hurry up, he'd be left behind. They'd played a good game that night, and Mike was tired and really looking forward to getting home.

The schedule had worked out well this year—their last game before the Christmas break was not only at home, but against Erik Larsson's team. This meant that they finally had a chance to have Erik, their friend and Alexei's ex, over for dinner. Usually they were lucky if they managed to sneak in a drink together before Erik or they were on the road again.

Mike wasn't going to leave their guest lingering in the hallway outside their locker room all afternoon just because Alexei was gossiping about Christmas presents with Rupert and Callum.

Mike had to bite his lips to keep from laughing when another bout of furious whispering broke out on the other side of the room.

He'd seen the three of them standing with their heads together from the shower room and purposely hung back, hoping they'd wrap it up before the rest of the team started to wonder what the hell Mike was doing. He had no desire to ruin any surprises he had coming his way.

In fact, he had a big one of his own up his sleeve. It was going to be an interesting Christmas.

Glancing down at his bag, Mike checked that the front pocket was still zipped shut. As security measures went, it wasn't great, but he knew Alexei wouldn't find it there.

Mike didn't want Alexei to have any clue of what Mike had gotten him until he opened it on Christmas morning. He wished that was because Alexei was going to be so delighted, but Mike didn't have any such delusions. There was a very real chance Alexei would balk when he saw Mike's gift. And Mike was fully prepared to out-stubborn him about it.

Alexei might not want to admit it, but Mike knew in his heart this was a perfect gift for Alexei. And once they were done arguing about it and Mike got his way, Alexei was going to love it.

By the time Mike was fully dressed, Alexei was just stripping off the last of his gear. Mike peeked out the door when one of the guys left, shouting "Merry Christmas" as he went. Erik hovered just outside in the hallway.

Mike went over to Alexei's stall. "Erik's already waiting."

No one would think anything of it—how close he was, or that they spoke quietly. Everyone knew they were best friends. And most knew they lived together—though they likely assumed Mike had his own room. As far as Mike and Alexei knew, no one had figured out that they had been lovers for years. Though, as Mike caught Tim eyeing them, he did wonder if there were some who were starting to suspect.

It was remarkable how little that bothered Mike.

Callum and Rupert were gay, and so far out of the closet that their wedding had appeared in *People Magazine*. For the most part, though, their coming out hadn't caused nearly as much of a stir within the team or the league as Mike would have predicted beforehand.

Of course, that didn't mean he and Alexei could come out. Or would. Being players was different than being an owner, like Callum, or even the manager, like Rupert.

"I'll be ready in ten minutes," Alexei promised, grabbing his stuff for the shower. He stopped to look at Mike carefully. "Are you okay keeping him company until I'm done?"

Mike smiled. He and Erik hadn't exactly gotten off on the right foot when they'd first met a few years back. They'd both logged quite a few minutes in the penalty box that night thanks to Erik attempting to get Alexei's attention, and Mike making it very, very clear that Alexei was no longer on the market.

"Sure, I can hang with your ex for a while. Maybe we'll trade stories," Mike said quietly, but with a mischievous wink.

Alexei rolled his eyes. "If you didn't share them all when you got drunk together last season, I don't think they're going to come out now."

"We'll see," Mike murmured, bumping Alexei's shoulder on his way to the door. "You might want to hurry up, just in case," he called back a moment before the door shut.

Erik gave him a curious look. "Should I ask?"

Mike shook his head and pulled Erik in for a quick hug. "Probably not."

For all that Alexei had been playing it cool, he somehow managed to get his ass out to the hallway in under seven minutes. Mike didn't even try to hide his laughter.

Alexei didn't really have anything to worry about. Mike liked Erik just fine, and now that Erik had made it clear he respected their relationship and boundaries, Mike had no beef with him. That Erik had been dumb enough to walk away from Alexei made Mike almost feel sorry for him.

But then, that was to Mike's benefit in the end, so he also felt grateful Erik was that stupid. Mike couldn't stand going even a few days without seeing Alexei. The idea of leaving him forever made his stomach hurt.

The ride home was quick with Alexei driving. Mike sat in the back seat of the huge pick-up and let Erik ride shotgun, mostly so Erik got a good view as they pulled up to the huge rolling doors into what appeared to be a slightly run-down, unassuming warehouse. With a press of a button, the doors parted before them.

"What the fuck is this place?" Erik whispered in awe.

"Home," Mike said with a smile.

Alexei parked inside the huge, empty first floor and Mike jumped from the truck and grabbed their bags. He noticed that Callum's car wasn't there, and wondered where their neighbors had gone off to for the night.

Shrugging, he led Erik to the elevator, chatting about how Alexei had bought the building years ago and the plans they had in the works. He knew he was being a dork, talking about it so enthusiastically, but he loved giving tours of their unusual space. He shamelessly let his pride in Alexei's cleverness and their combined hard work show while their guest looked around in wonder.

He continued the tour when they got to the fourth floor,

waving at Callum and Rupert's door before leading Erik to theirs, the only other unit on the floor.

He threw open the door with enough of a flourish that Alexei smiled, his hand warm and comforting at the small of Mike's back.

"You're showing off," Alexei admonished, though Mike could see he didn't really mean it as a rebuke.

"I am. I can't help it."

Alexei moved in closer, subtly pinning Mike to the doorframe while Erik moved into the apartment and exclaimed over the high ceilings and brightly lit kitchen.

A shiver worked down Mike's spine.

"You aren't worried about Erik, are you?" Alexei asked quietly.

For a moment, Mike was far too distracted by the press of Alexei's hips to parse what he'd just said. Then it clicked.

"God, no," he said, his lips brushing Alexei's ear. "I'm not showing off because I feel threatened. I'm showing off because I love our home. I'm proud of it. And you."

Alexei pressed just a little closer. "Good," he murmured, then captured Mike's lips in a kiss.

For a long moment, Alexei lost himself in the taste and texture of Mike's lips. He might have stood there all night if he hadn't been subtly nudged back.

He arched an eyebrow at Mike, surprised. Normally, Alexei decided when these things began and ended.

Mike cast a pointed look toward the kitchen. When Alexei turned his head, he found Erik watching them.

A lick of nerves tickled down Alexei's spine, along with a frisson of anticipation. This could work, but he had to convince Mike first.

"Come," he said brusquely, easing away from Mike a little. "Finish showing Erik around while I get us some beers."

Mike slid out from between Alexei and the door, his hand lingering on Alexei's hip as he went. Alexei smiled, perfectly attuned to all the subtle signs that Mike was aroused and how he tried to hide it.

Alexei grabbed the promised beverages, giving Mike time to finish the tour and show Erik to the couch, and himself a moment to press one of the bottles to his face, cooling his cheeks before going into the living room.

"Erik, if you're okay here for a minute, Mike and I will go drop our bags in the bedroom and get changed."

Mike looked at Alexei, his expression passive and accepting, and didn't ask why the hell he had to change out of his perfectly acceptable clothing.

Alexei fought to keep his expression bland and his dick down as he turned and walked away. Mike silently grabbed their bags and followed him into the bedroom, closing the door behind them.

"Come here, Michael," Alexei said in a low voice, watching Mike's cheeks warm to pink. Mike didn't hesitate, coming to stand so close, Alexei had to tilt Mike's chin down to see into his face.

Without a word, Alexei pulled open his bedside table drawer, his eyes never leaving Mike's. He saw how Mike's pupils dilated, how pink turned to red, high on Mike's cheekbones. Alexei needed only to stroke his fingers over a few items in the drawer before pulling out the brand-new toy he'd purchased just for this occasion.

Mike's eyes flicked to Alexei's hand, widened, then came back to Alexei's and stayed steady.

"Is this okay?" Alexei asked.

"Yes."

"Are you sure?" Because Alexei liked to be in charge, but he needed to be sure he was operating within Mike's comfort zone. Or, really, only making Mike uncomfortable in ways that Mike enjoyed, a favorite pastime for them both.

"Yes."

16

Alexei smiled. "Turn around and put your hands on the bed."

Mike did, instantly. Alexei indulged himself, running his hand down the long, strong line of Mike's back, rubbing the one sore spot that had been plaguing Mike all season until the tension eased from Mike's shoulders. Then Alexei knelt, reached around to open Mike's jeans, and tugged them and his boxer briefs down to his hips.

"Now, Michael, you have to be silent."

Mike sucked in a deep breath and nodded quickly, possibly not even aware of how he arched his back, canting his ass toward Alexei.

There was no way Alexei could stop himself from biting it. Hard.

Mike whimpered, a happy sound that forced Alexei to press the heel of his palm to his own dick and take a deep, shuddering breath through the teeth still clamped around all that tempting muscle and skin.

He released his bite and watched the blood rush to fill in each dent his teeth had left behind. He gently ran his hand over the mark.

"It will be faded before our next game," he promised Mike softly.

"I don't care."

Alexei pressed a gentle kiss to the mark and stood. Mike should care. They both should. And yet, apparently, they didn't. What did that mean about how hard they worked to keep this secret?

Alexei poured lube over his finger and put away the question for now. It wasn't one they were going to answer tonight. Tonight they were going to have a lovely dinner with a friend who knew not only that they were lovers, but was intimately familiar with Alexei's brand of loving.

With that in mind, he slipped the tip of one finger over Mike's tight hole, circling only once before pushing in. Mike's hands curled into the comforter so he could push back, taking Alexei's thick digit until the third knuckle was lodged against his

17

body. Mike's head dropped, hanging between his shoulders, his breathing already fast and speeding up more when Alexei tucked the second in right next to the first.

"We must be quick. I don't want to leave Erik waiting too long," Alexei said, smiling when Mike pushed back against his fingers and rolled his hips.

Alexei could feel the strength of the muscles clamping down on him, but also how they gave, softening to his touch and the pressure Mike was creating with each swivel of his body.

Alexei knew all the cues Mike's body could offer, and Mike knew Alexei would be looking for them.

The third finger drew a tiny, almost inaudible moan from Mike's throat. The stretched muscles clamped and fluttered around Alexei's fingers, trying to accommodate how quickly he was opening Mike up. It wasn't until they'd settled, still tight but no longer reacting to his every movement, that Alexei withdrew his hand and slicked up the heavy black butt plug he'd selected earlier. It was different than any of the others they'd played with in the past, the neck wider. The stretch would be constant and big. Mike was going to love it.

He didn't have to ask if Mike was ready. He could see it in the way Mike settled against the bed, widening his legs as much as the clothing bunched around his hips would allow. Could hear it in Mike's long, slow exhalation.

Alexei pressed the tip of the plug against Mike's hole and started to push. Erik had been on his own too long as it was, but Alexei wasn't going to hurry.

Mike, however, was done waiting. He shifted backwards and twisted his hips, seating himself on the plug Alexei held in a firm grip.

"Jesus Christ, Michael."

Mike lifted himself slowly to stand and Alexei reached out to steady him, running his hands over his ribs and holding his waist when he turned to face Alexei.

"I didn't want to be rude," Mike explained, his voice like gravel, his tone utterly sincere.

Alexei huffed out a laugh and helped him tug his clothing back into place. He slipped his hand into Mike's jeans before he could fasten the button, pressing where he knew the skin still smarted from the bite, then nudging the plug once.

Mike gasped and gripped Alexei's arms, his legs wobbling beneath him.

"You going to be able to manage this?" Alexei asked, more curious than concerned. Mike knew very, very well that he was never to put himself at risk or do anything he didn't want to do.

"I want it."

"Want what?"

"I want to sit and have a pleasant dinner with your ex, and be this excruciatingly aware of what he's missing. To know that you give me the best fucking Christmas presents and that, even better, the moment he leaves, you'll pull this thing out of me and do...god, I don't even know what. And I don't care, because I know I'll love it and I want to do whatever you want."

Alexei smiled and didn't correct Mike's assumptions. It was close enough to the truth, anyway, and Alexei was looking forward to teasing Mike with the rest.

Chapter Two

Dinner that night proved...challenging. Mike was gung-ho and helpful when he and Alexei returned to the kitchen to start making dinner, busying himself with setting out appetizers while Alexei worked on prepping the meal.

No one commented on the fact that Mike and Alexei had gone to the bedroom to change and come back fifteen minutes later in the exact same clothes. Though Erik's smirk would seem to indicate that fact hadn't escaped his notice.

Mike told himself to pretend it was just another night at home. It wasn't easy. He knew, at least, that he wasn't walking funny. Much. He and Alexei had played this particular game enough times that he was getting pretty good at not walking as if he felt like he had a giant knot in his ass, even when he did. If he wiggled a little when no one was looking, gasping at the jolts that fired off, then no one needed to know.

Except Alexei, who always seemed to catch him at it. And, well, maybe he wasn't as discreet as he thought, given the strange look on Erik's face all through their meal. But Erik couldn't possibly know *why* Mike was being weird. Erik had never been into the kinkier games, according to Alexei. There had to be another reason Erik kept watching Mike so intently, his eyes tracing over Mike's face, studying the color Mike knew was on his cheeks.

At one point Mike went to refill the water pitcher and thought he caught Erik checking out his junk, but it was so quick, he decided he must have been imagining it. It was hard enough to focus on the tasks before him without worrying about that.

As soon as dinner was over, they moved to the living room. Alexei sat right next to Mike on the sofa, while Erik took the deep armchair across from them. They sipped their coffees and chatted about their teams, the league, and the latest player gossip. Mike tried to pay attention, but he was faced with the dual challenge of finding a comfortable way to sit that didn't make it obvious how fucking good it felt to shift his weight, *and* the constant distraction of Alexei's hand as it traveled in a slow path up and down his thigh.

The heat in Mike's face told him his blush had deepened, and he fought to keep his breathing slow and even.

When Alexei's hand travelled even higher on the next pass, Mike squirmed, a small, almost pained noise escaping his throat as the plug glanced off his prostate.

It was safe to say he was no longer fooling anyone. Alexei kept the conversation going, and Erik played along, but even as their guest chatted with Alexei, his eyes were on Mike. Mike was so absorbed by what was happening to, and in, his body, it took him a while to notice what was happening to Erik's. When he finally pulled his head together enough to pay proper attention to their visitor, he was struck by the high color in *Erik's* cheeks. And the way he, too, was shifting in his seat.

In fact, he looked as turned on as Mike felt.

Erik was probably trying to be subtle when he adjusted himself, but Mike's eyes were drawn to the movement of Erik's hand. Mike blinked, wondering if he was having some sort of strange, arousal-induced hallucination. He *had* to be imagining just how...*much*...there was going on down there in Erik's pants.

He jumped, then gasped, when Alexei's hand tucked between his thighs and nudged up against his balls. His already partially hard dick went rigid.

"You okay, Michael?"

Michael.

Alexei only ever called him that when things turned intimate. When they were having sex, or dancing around some prelude to it, or snuggled up afterwards. When Alexei was in charge.

Mike looked at Alexei, who caught his gaze and held it. Waiting.

It took Mike's brain, swimming in endorphins, a moment to recall Alexei had asked him a question. "Yes, I'm okay."

"Good," Alexei said gently, squeezing Mike's thigh.

Mike glanced at Erik, then back at Alexei. His heart rate doubled as he figured out where this was going. He was pretty sure that this was turning into a threesome thing. Scratch that, he was pretty sure that Alexei had *arranged* a threesome. With Erik. Alexei's *ex-boyfriend.*

What Mike wasn't at all sure about was how he felt about that.

The concept of a threesome wasn't a new one for them. Alexei had made such arrangements in the past, a few times. And, god knew, Mike had loved every minute of those experiences. One particularly memorable Valentine's Day gift had involved visiting a sweet, slender man in Montreal who'd had the finest bones in his wrists. And fist. And knew just what to do with them.

Mike shuddered and glanced at Erik again, who stared back, silent and unmoving. Mike's eyes darted to Erik's lap, stalling when he saw how Erik's thick fingers were curled over his jeans, cupping his...

That couldn't all be his cock. Seriously.

Arousal curled up Mike's spine. He bit his cheek to keep from asking Alexei's permission to fall to his knees and crawl between Erik's legs. Just to look. To *see.*

He racked his brain, trying to remember if Alexei had ever mentioned Erik being particularly blessed in the dick department. There might have been a throw-away comment here or there. But there was also the more telling fact—one that Mike had never really considered the significance of before—that Alexei had never let Erik fuck him.

Mike was a shameless size queen, but Alexei most certainly was not. He liked a finger or two, sometimes even three or Mike's cock. But he wasn't like Mike. He didn't crave the stretch. The burn and triumph of forcing his body to accept something that filled him completely, until he could barely breathe for how good it felt.

And, well, it *was* Christmas.

Mike looked at Alexei and waited.

Alexei saw how Mike stared at him, patiently waiting for Alexei's word, whatever that might be.

It was moments like these that Alexei was more keenly aware than ever that he would give Mike anything.

The sun. The moon. *Erik.*

"Michael," he said carefully, trying to strike the right balance between being in command and making it very clear that Mike was the one with all the choices right now. He could see just a hint of hesitation in Mike's expression, and they would go no further unless whatever concerns Mike had were put to rest. He pulled one of Mike's hands into his lap and pressed it to the top of his thigh, laying his own hand over it. He needed the connection. He needed Mike to feel connected to *him.*

"I'd like to show you something."

Mike cocked his head. "Okay."

Alexei turned to Erik, dropping his voice to one of pure command. He and Erik had already negotiated this thoroughly. "Take it out."

Erik unzipped his jeans and shoved them down, then curled his fingers around his enormous cock, holding it up for their inspection as he drew his fist down the considerable length and girth.

Alexei carefully kept the delight off his face. Erik might actually be bigger than he remembered.

"Wow," Mike whispered almost reverently.

Erik released his grip and let his cock fall to his thigh with a thump.

Alexei rolled his eyes. *Show off.*

Mike swallowed hard, his hand clamped painfully around Alexei's thigh.

"Do you remember, Michael," Alexei began slowly, amused by Mike's inability to look away from Erik's lap, "the first time I fucked you? Do you remember what you told me?"

Mike shook his head.

"I commented that I wasn't as big as some of your toys," Alexei reminded him, smiling at the memory, well aware that Erik was even larger than most of those toys, "and you said I was better because I could move of my own volition."

Mike nodded, smiling a little, too. "I do remember that."

"Erik can do that, too."

"Move of his own volition?" Mike asked vaguely.

"No. Of *mine*."

Mike turned to look at him, his pupils blown so wide his brown eyes were almost entirely black. Erik started stroking himself again in Alexei's peripheral vision. He could hear Erik breathing faster.

Any sign of hesitation was lost from Mike's expression, subsumed by the desire Alexei could read a thousand ways in Mike's expression and posture. But that didn't mean there wasn't still room for regret, once it was over.

He cupped Mike's cheek. "Michael, I love you."

"I love you, too," Mike said immediately.

Alexei smiled and ran his thumb along Mike's cheekbone. Alexei wondered if decades from now, he'd stop wondering how he got so fucking lucky. "And I know that my history with Erik is probably on your mind." Mike nodded once. "So, Erik will not touch me. And I won't touch him, unless it's to help him fuck you properly. Just the way you want."

Mike's lips parted and he sucked in a huge breath, but his gaze remained fixed on Alexei as he nodded.

Erik sat forward, eagerly, but Alexei lifted a hand to still him and continued to study Mike. He and Mike both knew that wasn't enough.

Mike pressed his cheek into Alexei's palm and smile. "Yes," he said in a clear, calm voice.

Any remaining tension bled from Alexei's shoulders.

Alexei turned to Erik and lifted one eyebrow. "Strip."

Erik stood and yanked at his clothes, baring himself within seconds. Mike's grip on Alexei's thigh didn't loosen one iota as Erik's lean, long limbs came into view. Somehow all that whipcord strength only seemed to emphasize the length and breadth of his cock, making it incongruous. Anyone looking at Erik would expect him to be long and thin all over, but he was most decidedly *not*.

His cock hung between his legs, too heavy to lift like a lot of guys' would when fully erect. He was cut, the thick, pink head exposed and remarkably tempting. Alexei wouldn't be the one to indulge in that temptation, though.

He shoved the coffee table to the side with his foot, clearing a path between the couch and Erik. Erik didn't move, though. He knew better. The look he sent Alexei reminded him of how hard he'd chafed against Alexei's desire to be in charge when they were together. Back then, Erik had agreed to it, freely—just as he had tonight—but he'd never really settled into it.

Alexei wondered how he hadn't seen that at the time as clearly as he did now. He'd thought it was normal. Now, he looked at how Mike held himself still, staring and obviously eager, but waiting for Alexei to say or do something. To tell him what to do. And looking so fucking content with it.

Alexei would give him anything he wanted. To a degree he found almost frightening—until moments like this that reminded him they were perfect for each other, and he was the luckiest son of a bitch ever.

He touched Mike's cheek, bringing his face around to look at Alexei, and kissed him. In that instant, Erik was gone. His giant cock was forgotten. It was only them. Mike shifted, leaning closer and groaning as their tongues tangled and the plug in his ass no doubt shifted in interesting ways.

Mike's breathing sped up, his grip on Alexei's leg bruising.

Alexei pulled back. "You can touch him, if you want," he said to Mike.

Mike immediately slid to his knees, then paused to look back at Alexei.

"Yes, your mouth, too."

Erik shifted, swaying on his feet slightly before settling with his feet planted further apart, as if bracing for a hit. Alexei almost laughed. Erik had no fucking idea.

Mike crawled to Erik, stopping just a few inches away to stare at Erik's cock and licking his lips in contemplation.

Erik looked at Alexei, his eyes pleading, but Alexei shook his head once. If Mike wanted to stare for an hour, he could. It was his time to play.

Erik was so busy shooting daggers at Alexei, he jumped when a hand wrapped about his thick shaft and tugged experimentally.

Alexei smirked at how both Erik and Mike's eyes widened comically.

Mike looked up at Erik. "Dude, you're huge."

Erik smiled. "Yes," he said without a whiff of self-consciousness or humility.

Alexei rolled his eyes again. Erik could be insufferably arrogant, even if in this case, he had cause. He wasn't fooling Alexei with his nonchalant response, though. Alexei could see how Erik's jaw flexed, his fingers dug into his palms. Erik was wound tighter than a spring.

He wasn't the only one, either. Alexei decided to take a little mercy on them all. His own cock was aching in his jeans from being mildly turned on all through dinner, and fully erect since Mike had fallen to his knees. He could only imagine how Mike's cock must feel.

"Michael," Alexei said in a smooth voice.

Mike looked at him over his shoulder, his eyes bright and his lips wet from licking them. Now Alexei slid to the floor, too, inexorably drawn to Mike. He knee-walked closer, until he could thread his knees between Mike's and wrap his hands around Mike's hips. Then he sat back on his heels and drew Mike onto his lap.

Mike gasped and ground against Alexei, his chin tipped up

and mouth open as he jammed the plug into himself and worked it there.

"Do you want to taste him?" he murmured into Mike's ear.

Beyond words, Mike nodded quickly and Alexei shot Erik a stern look. "Feed him your cock." When Erik grabbed his dick and leaned forward, Alexei stilled him with one hand on his thigh. "Just the tip."

Erik brushed the head of his cock against Mike's lips and Mike's tongue came out, as if to receive the unholiest of communions. It curled around the shiny, dark-pink skin, tracing the crown gently before pulling it into his mouth.

Erik groaned, long and loud, his hands flailing at his sides, looking for something to grab onto. He knew he wasn't allowed to touch Mike or Alexei without permission.

"Clasp your hands behind your back, Erik," Alexei said firmly. Erik actually listened, his hips canting forward in the process.

Mike moaned and took a few inches of the shaft into his mouth, his chin dropping and lips stretching to accommodate Erik's girth.

Erik swayed before them.

"Michael, I'm going to hold Erik's thighs to help him stay still for you, okay?" Alexei asked quietly.

Mike was in no position to give verbal agreement, but he grabbed Alexei's hands and placed them on Erik, making his consent clear enough.

"If you want him to move, that's okay, too," Alexei added in a low whisper.

Mike whimpered around Erik's shaft, but didn't indicate anything else, so Alexei just braced Erik and let Mike set the pace.

Soon his head was bobbing, his whole body leaning into each plunge to take more of Erik's cock into his mouth, each retreat planting him more firmly in Alexei's lap and ending with a small, shaky circle of his hips. His hands gripped Alexei's thighs, reassuring Alexei that Mike would be able to get Alexei's attention and tap out if needed.

Erik's mouth hung open as he sucked in great lungfuls of air, apparently transfixed by the sight of his cock disappearing into Mike's mouth. Alexei couldn't blame him. It was a fairly hypnotizing sight.

Mike had managed to take in maybe half of Erik's length before he gagged and retreated quickly.

Alexei let go on one of Erik's legs and threaded his fingers into Mike's hair. "You can do better than that, Michael."

He watched carefully, gauging Mike's reaction, smiling when Mike immediately plunged again, his head tipped back further. Alexei tightened his grip on Mike's head and gently urged him forward. Mike's hands never left Alexei's thighs, never once giving any indication he might tap out, as Alexei tipped him forward and Erik's thick shaft lodged in the back of Mike's throat.

Mike swallowed once, his eyes fluttering closed and his cheeks heating to scarlet. Alexei eased him back immediately.

"Again?"

Mike's only answer was to lean forward, eagerly, and lift his chin higher.

"Jesus fucking Christ," Erik said in a ragged voice above them, his abdominal muscles clenching tight as he stared down at them with wide, wild eyes. Alexei wondered if Erik recognized he'd said that in Swedish.

But mostly he concentrated on easing Mike forward, lifting to keep their hips grinding together, to keep working the plug in Mike's ass while his throat was filled with Erik's cock.

Tears leaked from Mike's eyes, but Alexei wasn't concerned. In fact, he was elated. Mike looked like he was in heaven.

He swallowed again, several times, and pulled a string of curses from Erik that ended with a guttural growl. Alexei was so fixated on Mike and his pleasure, he was surprised when a hand tapped his on Erik's thigh.

Alexei sat back immediately, pulling Mike with him. The moment Erik's cock slipped free of Mike's mouth, Mike let out a needy, disappointed sound.

Erik swore again.

"Michael, Erik needed to take a break," Alexei explained while checking Erik over to be sure he wasn't somehow hurt. A steady stream of precome pearled on the head of Erik's cock before dripping off. Mike caught each drop on his tongue without touching Erik.

Alexei looked up at Erik. "Too close?" he guessed.

"Yes."

Erik had been given strict orders not to come until and unless Alexei told him to. It was a command he'd often ignored in the past.

"Thank you," Alexei said, acknowledging how hard Erik was trying.

Erik looked a little bewildered. "I don't want to disappoint him," he admitted quietly.

Alexei pressed his face to the pounding pulse in Mike's throat and smiled. It was somehow sweet and reassuring that he wasn't the only one who Mike could do this to.

He pulled the soft skin against his lips between his teeth and sucked, knowing it would make Mike squirm in his lap. Alexei's cock was so hard that he was a little worried it was going to be damaged permanently if he didn't get it out of his jeans soon.

Releasing his bite with a soft pop, he brushed his cheek along Mike's until they were both staring at Erik's cock from an inch away, Mike's tongue still darting out to catch drops of precome, licking them directly from the skin. Erik's dick twitched and swayed with each contact.

"What do you want to do now, Michael?"

"I want him to fuck me."

Chapter Three

Mike sat in Alexei's lap, staring at Erik's honestly ginormous dick, and waited for Alexei to tell him what to do next. It was almost impossible not to rub his ass against Alexei's legs, so he didn't bother trying to hold still. He figured not outright bouncing up and down on the plug was restraint enough.

He wasn't even a little bit concerned about his request for Erik to fuck him. He was pretty sure that was the whole point of this thing, and even if it weren't, Alexei would tell him what to do. Mike knew that whatever Alexei *did* want would be nothing short of mind-blowing.

Alexei's arms curled around his waist and he leaned back. When Alexei spoke, Mike could feel the vibrations from his voice through his back where it was pressed to Alexei's chest.

"Erik, sit down."

Erik did. Immediately. But he also sent Alexei a questioning look, clearly trying to figure out what was going to happen next. Mike almost shook his head. Erik should trust Alexei. After all the time they were together, he should *know* Alexei would take good care of them both.

The more Mike got to know Erik, the more Alexei and Erik's break-up made sense. And not just like this. It was obvious Erik would never understand Alexei. And could never appreciate the joy that could be found in just giving himself over.

"Michael," Alexei said against his cheek. "Let's get you undressed."

Mike nodded and stood gingerly. The moment he was steady on his feet, he stripped off his shirt while Alexei went to work opening his jeans. Mike shoved them down and kicked off his shoes and socks quickly.

Alexei then rose and stripped down, too. Mike watched him, saw how he overbalanced to protect his hips while lifting his legs, and wondered how he could feel so much love, so much affection, and so *annoyed* at the same time. The stubborn man would not admit his hips now hurt constantly during the hockey season.

Mike reached out and drew his hand down the length of Alexei's erection, pleased to feel the proof of how affected Alexei was by all this, too. Sometimes Alexei did things purely for Mike's benefit, which was fine. Fucking great, really. But Mike preferred it when they both got off on whatever they were doing. He wanted tonight to be like that.

Alexei kissed him, once, and it was fierce and far too brief. Then he looked Erik over, appraisingly, and nodded once.

"Michael, Erik likes your mouth too much," he said, sounding regretful. Mike was pleased to hear it, though. "But I think you should spend more time getting to know him while I get you ready."

Mike nodded, shivering with anticipation for the "getting ready" part, but knew to wait for the rest of whatever Alexei was going to say. There would be rules. Limits. Mike *wanted* those. He didn't want to have to decide what was right.

"You can put your mouth on him, but you can't put him in your mouth. Do you understand?"

"Yes."

Alexei smiled and ran a hand down Mike's back as he knelt between Erik's knees. Erik spread his legs until his thighs pressed to the arms of the chair, his tongue caught between his teeth as he stared down at Mike hungrily.

Alexei left the room, but Mike knew he'd be back soon.

He rested his cheek against the inside of one of Erik's thighs and stared up at his cock, resting on his stomach. Mike's ass clenched at the thought of all of that being inside of him. He *wanted* that.

Nuzzling his face to the coarse hair and smooth skin, he worked his way up Erik's thigh, switching to the other when it became too difficult to move because of his own broad shoulders and the limitation of the chair's arms. When he came to a stop, just a few inches shy of Erik's balls, Erik groaned. Mike sucked warm skin into his mouth and drew blood to the surface, shifting with Erik when he squirmed in the seat. It wasn't until a foot struck Mike's shoulder that he pulled away and realized Erik had hooked his knee over the arm of the chair, opening himself to Mike.

"Sorry," Erik gasped, his foot swinging away.

Mike smiled and ran his hands up both Erik's thighs until they framed his cock and balls, his thumbs pressing into the meat of Erik's ass. He pulled the cheeks apart and gently rubbed the swirl of tight muscles around Erik's hole while he bent to mouth the length of Erik's shaft.

Erik, apparently, was loud when he was really turned on. Mike had been too busy trying to inhale his cock earlier to really notice, but now he could hear the gasps and pleas and even grunts of pleasure as Mike teased him mercilessly.

Erik wasn't loud enough, though, to mask the unmistakable sound of a cap clicking open behind Mike.

Mike lifted his ass in the air, putting his hands on Erik's thighs to support and stabilize himself while he licked over Erik's tight sac, teasing each ball into his mouth to massage with his tongue and lips before releasing it to start all over again on the other side. He buried his nose in the coarse hair around the base of the shaft and inhaled, reveling in the scent of musk and sweat.

He shuddered when Alexei's hand brushed over his ass. He'd been so distracted by the bounty before him, he'd almost forgotten about the plug. Not now, though. Not when Alexei curled his fingers around the base and tugged, opening Mike up before pushing it back in again.

Mike moaned his approval as Alexei began to fuck the plug in and out of him. Long, firm strokes that sent chills up Mike's spine each time his ass stretched to accommodate the full breadth of it, then clenched closed around the narrow neck, then stretched again as Alexei twisted it from his body. He panted against Erik's belly, his cheek pressed to his shaft, his breath gusting over the head.

Erik squirmed beneath him, his other leg hooking over the other arm of the chair. Mike leaned back to appreciate the view, sucking in a deep breath when Alexei forced the plug back into his ass and ground it up into him. His eyes fluttered closed and for a moment, all he could do was ride the waves of sensation streaking through his body.

God, that was good. And he was getting close. Too close.

He needed a distraction. Immediately.

As much as he wanted to stay right where he was, he forced himself to tip forward again. He nuzzled along Erik's shaft and licked at the head of his cock, reminding himself to breathe as best he could while Alexei continued to torment him with the plug.

The taste of precome exploded over his tongue, telling him he wasn't the only one enjoying what Alexei was doing to him. He focused there, on that taste, gasping against the sensitive skin when Alexei tugged the plug from him one last time and it landed with a thud next to his leg.

Mike glanced down to see the towel Alexei had spread over the rug around him. When had that happened?

He discarded that trivial concern when two fingers slipped into his body, testing the already well-used muscles of his anus. The third finger barely registered, Mike was so open. So ready.

He didn't bother to tell Alexei to hurry. It wouldn't do any good, and it might just make him slow down. Mike contented himself with torturing Erik as best he could within the limits set by Alexei. He tickled his tongue behind Erik's balls, testing the seam of skin there, and Erik slid further down the chair, forcing himself against Mike's tongue in a blatant invitation for Mike to go further.

Mike moved back to Erik's shaft, smiling at Erik's disappointed whine. Mike liked to rim Alexei, and god knew he loved it when Alexei rimmed him, but that wasn't something they shared with other people. That was just between them, and that's how Mike liked it.

He moaned against Erik's shaft when Alexei spread his

fingers, stretching him wide. His legs shook, his cock dripping onto the towel, and he shoved himself back against that delicious pressure. He thought about reaching down to grab his dick to try to force back the building need fueled by the anticipation of getting Erik into him at last. The thought was lost, along with any others, when Alexei pinched the fresh bite mark on Mike's right cheek.

He keened, high and needy.

Alexei leaned in close and whispered in his ear. "He's big, Mike."

"I noticed," Mike gasped between pants.

"How much do you want to feel it?"

Mike considered his answer, knowing Alexei wouldn't accept anything less than the truth, but too far gone into his own head to be able to know what that was without giving it some concerted thought. Once he had, though, he knew what he wanted.

"I want to feel it. A lot. I want it to be like Montreal."

Alexei's hand slipped away and he stood. "Come," he said, putting a gentle hand under Mike's arm and helping him to stand.

Mike's legs felt like Jell-O, but he managed to stay upright with Alexei's help. Erik, apparently, was on his own.

"Follow us," Alexei said as he grabbed the towel, and whatever was wrapped up in it, and turned toward the kitchen.

Mike had thought they might use the couch, or the coffee table, but of course, Alexei knew better. They would have been too low, and made it harder for Erik to thrust as hard as Mike would want him to. *Need* him to.

Mike shivered as he stood in the middle of the kitchen, Erik standing a few feet away as they both watched Alexei carefully clean off the long rectangular table at which they'd just eaten dinner. Alexei laid the towel across the head of the table and set two chairs by the legs on either side.

Alexei then hopped up on the table, his ass perched on the

towel and at the very edge of the hard, flat surface. He planted his feet on the chairs, which were far enough apart that his legs were spread almost impossibly wide.

"Goalies," Erik muttered behind Mike.

Mike smiled and held Alexei's gaze.

"Come here, Michael."

Mike went to stand between Alexei's legs, his hands resting on Alexei's thighs as he smiled down at his amazing, generous boyfriend.

"Will this be okay for you?" Alexei asked.

"Yes."

Alexei looked over Mike's shoulder. "Erik, come here." Mike felt the heat radiating from Erik a moment before his cock brushed Mike's ass and a hand landed on his hip. "You're going to fuck Michael now, exactly as I tell you to. Is that okay?"

Alexei's eyes narrowed on Erik. Mike could guess from the small movements behind him that Erik was nodding.

"We use our words, Erik. The right words, unless you don't want to do this. Then you can go."

With a great sigh, Erik finally said, "Yes, Alexei. I want to do this. I consent."

Mike arched an eyebrow, wondering if Alexei would do anything about Erik's sass, but Alexei just smiled and pulled Mike closer. His kiss was gentle, his tongue slipping between Mike's lips for just a taste before he retreated and skimmed his lips along Mike's cheekbone. When Alexei's mouth brushed Mike's ear, he whispered, in Russian, "There are so many reasons I love you, my perfect boy. He's but a pale shadow in your light, and not worth my time. This is about you and what you want."

Mike shivered again, his eyes slipping closed as he pressed his cheek to Alexei's and slid his arms around his ribs, cherishing his warmth, his steady presence, his generosity.

"I love you, too," Mike said in Russian.

Alexei kissed him just behind the ear, nuzzling him for a moment, then lay back on the table. Mike knew that at least a quarter of that bright smile was because of Mike's horrible accent, but another half or more was because Mike's attempts to learn Russian delighted Alexei.

Alexei nudged Mike to the side and held out a hand. "Erik, for you."

Erik took the bottle of lube and condom from Alexei, and Mike was careful to remain out of the line of sight so that Alexei could watch Erik put the condom on. They wouldn't be here at all if Alexei didn't trust Erik with this, but Mike knew Alexei had to be certain, had to *see* that Mike would be completely safe.

Mike wondered if there was something wrong with him that something that should have been kind of hot—and maybe a little kinky—just warmed him and made his heart hurt with how much he loved his boyfriend.

Maybe that was obvious in his smile as he looked down at Alexei, the tenderness reflected in Alexei's eyes as he towed Mike closer again. Mike sighed as their erections slid together and he bent over and planted his hands on the table on either side of Alexei's shoulders.

Alexei kept tugging him closer and Mike happily lay down on top of him, capturing his mouth in a long, hot kiss. He could do this for hours. Days, even. Alexei's tongue twined with his, his hands smoothing over Mike's shoulders and down his back, rubbing over his spine and hips, warming him and easing the tension from his muscles.

Mike gasped, though, when Alexei's fingers dug into his ass cheeks and pulled them apart. Mike spread his feet, planting them more firmly on the floor.

Erik didn't need any more prompting than that. Almost immediately, two fingers slipped into Mike's ass.

"I'm ready," he groaned, way beyond wanting more preparation. He was ready. *Now.*

"Shhhh..." Alexei murmured against his lips. "Erik insisted he should know how you felt, how tight you were. He's only being careful, Michael."

Mike could see how a guy hung like Erik would have to set

some rules for himself, when it came to new lovers. He tried to be patient, but the feeling of Erik gently testing his already lax muscles, tugging against his rim before opening him up with both his thumbs, was making him crazy. His knees shook and he locked them, leaning more of his weight onto Alexei's chest. Alexei still had his hands full of Mike's ass, so Mike took advantage and dragged his palms down Alexei's ribs. Nibbled along his jaw and sucked his earlobe between his lips.

Alexei shifted beneath him and they both hissed, their cocks bumping and sliding between their bodies.

"Please, Erik," Mike begged, his voice hoarse.

Erik's hands left him, almost immediately replaced by a blunt, wide pressure against his hole that Mike could guess was Erik's cock. It felt...*big.* Bigger even than Mike had been expecting.

Which was fucking fantastic.

When Erik didn't move, didn't press forward, Mike groaned with frustration.

"I'm ready, Alexei," Erik said.

Mike swallowed an exasperated sigh. Apparently the damn man could play by the rules when it suited him.

Alexei's grip changed, and now it was *his* fingers pulling Mike's rim wide. Mike arched his back into the pressure, his neck stretched, chin high, as he hovered there, waiting for what came next.

"Push," said Alexei, and Mike had no idea if Alexei was speaking to him or to Erik, but they both responded. Mike bore down as Erik thrust forward and stretched Mike open, tight muscles he'd been sure were loose enough burning as his body fought to reject Erik's cock even as he rejoiced in the desire to accept it.

He'd had this cock in his mouth. Against his lips. He'd thought he'd known exactly how big it was, but it felt bigger, harder, and heavier as the head pushed against him and Alexei's fingers pulled him open.

He whimpered, a needy sound torn from his throat. He'd had

toys this big in him. And a fist, once. But this was different. He could feel the heat of the blood rushing beneath Erik's skin, hear the desperate edge to the noises Erik made, and knew he was as turned on as Mike.

The stretch in his ass was so consuming, he couldn't even respond to the feeling of Alexei's body rubbing along his cock as Mike writhed against him. All Mike wanted, all he cared about, was getting Erik inside him.

The head popped past his rim and he shuddered hard. Goddamn, that was fucking *perfect.*

Alexei and Erik both chuckled. Apparently, he'd said that out loud.

"Push," Alexei said again, and this time Mike knew it wasn't for him. He was beyond that kind of control anyway. All he could do was dig his fingers into Alexei's arms and hold the fuck on as Erik slowly sank further, opening him up and dragging along his inner walls. Mike's knees almost buckled when that big, fat head brushed over his prostate and kept going, the shaft then skimming over it with a constant pressure that made Mike's head spin.

Fuck. That was—it was—he felt a flair of panic. He wasn't going to last long. Goddamn it. He couldn't...

"Michael, look at me."

Mike's eyelids felt heavy as he dragged them open and stared down into Alexei's face. Whatever Alexei saw made his concerned expression morph into a smirk. "That good?" he asked teasingly.

Mike swallowed hard but still couldn't speak. He nodded.

"Don't come," Alexei said sternly.

Mike whimpered again. Hearing that, as always, *didn't help.* Judging by the twinkle in Alexei's eyes, he knew it, too.

"Erik," Alexei said, almost conversationally. "You should fuck Michael now."

Erik grunted, his hips kicking and seating his cock to the hilt. Mike's eyes drifted closed again and he sucked a deep breath in through his nose.

"Now, Erik."

Mike thought he was ready, but he still cried out as Erik slowly withdrew, dragging that insanely wide and fucking wonderful shaft over his prostate, the head bouncing off it for an added jolt.

Mike shifted his feet to steady himself and clung to Alexei as he drowned in the sensations storming him. He heard the rude squelch of lube as Erik added more slick, felt it drip down his perineum and over his balls, but none of it detracted from the amazing feeling of being so *full* as Erik thrust back in. The stretch was awesome. The burn and ache of his rim exactly what he wanted.

A Christmas fucking miracle.

That might have been out loud, too, but Alexei stopped the stupid shit from pouring from his mouth by capturing it in a kiss. Mike hadn't even realized Alexei had let go of Mike's ass until his hands wrapped around his jaw and cheeks and held him steady as Erik's thrusts picked up speed and force.

Mike kissed Alexei back, furiously, incapable of stopping the noises being forced up from his chest with every thrust. His body slid over Alexei's, sweat easing the friction between them, his cock gliding along the crease between Alexei's hip and thigh, otherwise forgotten. Which was for the best, since it would take almost nothing to set him off.

Alexei tore his mouth away. "Spread your legs further," he coaxed, and Mike obeyed, his feet skittering across the floor. Alexei's hand pressed to his back. "Tilt your ass higher."

Mike did that, too, and howled as the full power of Erik's thrust nailed the head of his cock against Mike's prostate like a pile-driver.

"Harder, Erik," Alexei barked, his ears ringing from Mike's cries.

Erik listened. Alexei wasn't sure whose demands Erik was responding to, but it got the job done.

Soon Mike was panting against Alexei's neck, his fingers bruising Alexei's arms, his vocabulary honed down to just one word. Over and over.

"Please."

Alexei wanted to give his boy what he wanted, but he thought Mike would like it even better, enjoy it even more, if he waited just a little longer.

Also, Alexei was fucking dying to come, too. He raised his feet and planted his heels on the edge of the table, clamping Mike's ribs in his thighs and rolling his hips up to thrust his cock against Mike's trembling abs.

Alexei's hips jerked harder, faster, but it wasn't fucking enough. He thrust so hard his ass lifted off the table, the muscles in his thighs burning, and that was better. More friction, and Erik's ever-more-powerful thrusts moving them both.

Heat pooled at the base of his spine, tightening the muscles in his ass and thighs, which shook as he continued to thrust. He was about to reach down with one hand when Mike beat him to it, shoving his arm between them and curling his fingers around Alexei's aching cock.

Alexei came with a shout, his thighs squeezing Mike as he bucked up against him and spilled onto his own belly. Shockwaves of pleasure washed over him, whiting out his brain while Mike rocked above him from Erik's relentless fucking.

Alexei collapsed back onto the table. When he could manage to control his own limbs again, he pressed his hand low on Mike's back and brushed his lips against Mike's ear. "My boy," he whispered in hoarse Russian, knowing that Mike would be able to translate this much without effort. "Is this what you wanted?"

"Yes," he gasped.

"Are you close?"

Mike's only response was to whimper.

Alexei smiled. "Come."

Mike growled, his back arching as he shoved himself back on Erik's cock. Erik almost stumbled, grabbing Alexei's hips and driving forward until the three of them were slammed together. Alexei didn't need to hear Mike's howl of pleasure to imagine how that felt, to be so full and stretched so wide.

Mike's hands convulsed around his arms once, then his entire body went rigid and warmth spread across Alexei's belly.

Erik gasped. "Alexei, please."

Alexei jolted, a little ashamed of himself for forgetting about Erik. He just hadn't been able to think about anything but *Mike.*

"Yes, Erik. You, too."

Mike groaned when Erik continued to thrust into him. Alexei's head felt light just thinking about how sensitive Mike must be. How sore.

Erik shouted something in Swedish, too garbled for Alexei to decipher, and curled over Mike, his shoulders bowed and head hanging down as he shook, his hips grinding into Mike as he came.

Alexei lay on the table, still panting, as Mike slowly lifted his head and blinked down at him. Erik's hands left Alexei's hips and disappeared behind Mike a moment before Mike's eyes widened, his mouth dropping open. Erik slowly moved away, then stumbled toward the bathroom with a hand holding the condom in place.

Alexei brushed a hand over Mike's face, pushing his damp hair back from his forehead. "How do you feel?"

Mike smiled, though it was wobbly. "Great," he said.

Alexei slowly sat up, pushing Mike upright with him, before dropping his feet off the table and wincing as pain shot up his legs. Mike's hands went to his hips, offering warmth and pressure and relief.

Alexei grumbled. "I'm not too old to have good sex."

A grin flashed on Mike's face. "Obviously not."

"I will never be too old for good sex," he said firmly, to clarify.

"I should hope not," Mike said before kissing Alexei gently. Alexei leaned up, tracing his tongue over Mike's lips, intent on proving his point, but then Mike wavered on his feet.

Alexei caught him with an arm around his waist. "Come, let's get you to bed."

"I should see Erik out," Mike protested immediately.

Alexei laughed. "I'm sure he'll understand. You can make it up to him the next time we see him."

Mike was docile—more so than usual, even—as Alexei led him to their bedroom. Alexei quickly wiped them down and tucked Mike into bed. Mike's eyes were already closing by the time Alexei pulled the covers up to his shoulders. He bent to kiss Mike's cheek.

"I'll be back in a moment."

Mike murmured into the pillow and smiled. Alexei called for a cab and pulled on his robe before going back out to the kitchen.

Erik met him wearing his clothes, his jacket, and a terribly smug smile Alexei chose to ignore.

"Thank you," he said earnestly.

"I think that's my line," Erik said with a chuckle.

Alexei hugged him. "We're playing you again next month. Let's make time to get together."

"Like this? Or—"

"No. Not then. And maybe not again, ever," Alexei said honestly. "Mike and I have to talk before any plans are made in that direction."

"Of course." Erik appeared to think about what he wanted to say for a moment. "For what it's worth," he began hesitantly, "I'm glad we broke up if it means you get to be with Mike. He's perfect for you, isn't he?"

He was, Alexei thought, in far more ways than Erik would ever see or understand. He smiled gratefully and chose to ignore Erik's insinuation that he had, at some point, regretted dumping Alexei's ass all those years ago.

Alexei's phone chimed and he looked down at it. "Your cab is here."

"Not going to drive me to my hotel?" Erik asked, pretending to be put out.

Alexei opened the door. "No. Mike needs me." *And you don't come close to outranking that.* "Do you need help with the elevator?"

"Nah, I got it," Erik said with a good-natured smile and a last quick hug. "You go take care of your boy."

Alexei arched an eyebrow, but said nothing about Erik's choice of words. Erik didn't speak Russian, though, so it had to be a lucky guess. Alexei waited in the hall until the elevator closed before hurrying back to the bedroom. He stripped off his robe and climbed into bed, pulling Mike close until he lay boneless over Alexei's chest.

"Is Erik okay?" Mike murmured against his throat.

"Yes," Alexei said as he ran his hand down Mike's ribs and over his hip. Mike scooted closer, curling an arm around Alexei's torso and hitching one leg up over his hips.

Alexei smiled. He knew what Mike was asking for.

He kissed Mike gently and teased two fingers over his swollen rim. Mike shivered, quietly humming his pleasure. Alexei could only imagine how sore and sensitive the entire area was as he gathered what little lube was left after his clean up.

When Mike squirmed, as if trying to get even closer, Alexei pressed his fingers through the tight, hot ring of muscles.

"*Oh god.*"

"Good?"

"Yesss," Mike hissed.

Alexei was fairly impressed to feel Mike's cock start to harden against his hip. He began to plunge his fingers in and out of Mike's poor, abused hole.

Mike let out a huge sigh. "Thank you."

"For this?" Alexei asked with a smile, tugging at Mike's rim and making him shudder.

"No. Well, yes," he said, and Alexei could feel Mike's smile against his skin. "But also for tonight. Best Christmas present ever."

Alexei's hand froze until Mike mewled in protest. He resumed thrusting into Mike, teasing his rim with a third finger. Mike hitched his leg higher, opening himself up in an invitation Alexei had no intention of refusing. It was a tight fit.

Mike gasped, but it was a happy sound.

"Michael," Alexei asked curiously. "What exactly do you think was your Christmas present?"

Mike hummed contentedly. "You know," he said softly, though it sounded a little bit like a question.

Alexei chuckled and didn't bother to clarify.

Chapter Four

Mike woke up with a start, sprawled out across the bed on his stomach. He would have thought it was just a bad dream that caused him to wake if Alexei hadn't bolted upright in bed beside him.

Someone pounded on the door at the same moment that Mike's phone started to buzz on the nightstand.

Alexei put a hand on Mike's back before he jumped from the bed and tugged on his robe. "You stay here. I'll go see what's going on."

There were only so many people who knew where they lived, let alone how to get to their door, so Mike wasn't worried, per se. Though it wasn't like any of those people to beat down their door at—Mike reached for his phone—six o'clock in the morning. And on Christmas Eve—*a day off*—no less.

Mike was alarmed to see he'd already missed two calls from Rupert and three from Callum. He didn't bother to call either of them back, though, as he could just make out Rupert's voice through the bedroom door.

He sounded worked up about something.

Mike dropped his head back onto the pillow and gave himself a couple of minutes to wake up properly while he waited for Alexei to return. He'd been looking forward to having a long, lazy morning in bed, and was still holding out hope that it would be possible.

When Alexei came swinging through the bedroom door, already shrugging out of his robe on the way to the bathroom, that hope was extinguished.

"What's up?" Mike called after him.

"I'm not sure," Alexei admitted, his voice echoing against the tiles a moment before the shower turned on. He immediately returned to the bedroom, steam billowing out the door behind him. "Gabriel called, apparently, and Rupert and Callum need to go to Pathways. They asked if we could hang out with the boys until they get back."

Mike lifted his head from the pillow. "Is everything okay?" The Pathways Center was a local family and youth shelter and community center, and Gabriel its director. Mike and Alexei, along with Rupert and Callum and more and more of the Ice Cats organization, volunteered there often and knew the center, and its staff, well.

"Yes. I think so. Rupert seemed excited, at least, but I have no idea what about. I just agreed we'd get over there in the next half hour. We can make the kids breakfast."

Dreams of sleeping in and lazing in bed with Alexei gone, Mike nodded and climbed to his feet. He immediately swayed and reached for the bed post, but Alexei caught him first.

"Woah," Alexei said, wrapping his arms around Mike. "You okay?"

Mike huffed out a laugh. "Yeah," he said, a slow smile forming, "I'm great."

He'd woken up aware that his ass was sore, his rim hot and swollen. But he hadn't realized his legs would still shake, or that the heat would spread through him like this.

His cock twitched, filling, as he stood still and took stock of myriad aches and pains and delicious little pleasures.

Alexei glanced down, saw Mike's erection, and arched one eyebrow. Mike grinned. Goddamn, he felt *awesome*.

"Come," Alexei said. With a steadying hand on Mike's back, Alexei led him into the steamy bathroom and into the shower. The hot water felt fantastic, and Mike stepped directly under the spray, letting it pour over his head and splash onto Alexei as he wrapped his arms around Mike's waist and curled his hand around Mike's cock.

From there, it didn't take long. Just long enough for Alexei to thrust two fingers into Mike's aching hole and tap his prostate while stroking his fist along Mike's shaft. It was quick enough, in fact, to leave time for Mike to drop to his knees and show Alexei how very, very much Mike appreciated his Christmas gift from the night before.

As soon as they were done cleaning up, they pulled on some clothes and started out of the apartment. Alexei stopped Mike with a hand on his arm. "Do you want some cream?" Alexei asked, referring to the special ointment they kept for those times Mike needed to be able to play hockey—or do anything else— without the twinges from his ass.

Mike smiled. "No."

Today, he wanted to feel every second of it and savor his gift.

They let themselves into Rupert and Callum's apartment to find the usual chaos unfolding around them. Rupert was in the kitchen on the phone and pouring a cup of coffee, while his husband, Callum, was coming out of their bedroom with his head lost in the sweater he was pulling on. Their eldest, Christian, reached him just in time to prevent Callum from walking directly into a wall.

Christian rolled his eyes with the despair for a parent only a teenager could manage.

Callum's head popped through the neck hole. "Oh, hey, guys. Thanks for coming over so quickly."

"No problem," Mike said, peering over the back of the couch. As he'd suspected, Oliver was curled up under a blanket, zoning out with Curious George on the TV. He was getting a little old for the show, but it was still his favorite for when he was half asleep or stressed out. Mike studied his little face for a moment and determined this was the former.

"Oliver," he said, brushing his hand over the mop of dark, silky hair poking out of the blankets, "are you still going to help me later?"

Oliver smiled up at him. "I will, if you still need my help."

"I do," Mike promised. He just had to figure out when he was going to convince Alexei to go out and do the last of his holiday shopping now that their plans had been put into a bit of a tailspin. Mike needed Alexei gone long enough to wrap the last of his gifts, a task Mike had promised Oliver he could help with.

Mike glanced over at the enormous tree in the corner of the living room and smiled. It had all of Rupert and Callum's, *and* Mike and Alexei's, ornaments this year. With the travel schedule what it was, and Rupert and Callum's invitation to spend Christmas here with them, Mike and Alexei hadn't bothered to get a tree this year, opting instead to share one with the family across the hall.

Their family.

Mike startled when Rupert ran up and hugged him. "Thank you so much for being here," Rupert said, far more earnestly than last-minute childcare duties—which they did all the time—seemed to warrant.

"Always," Mike said automatically, because he had no idea what Rupert's deal was this morning and because it was true.

"Come on, duchess," Callum said patiently from the door.

Rupert grinned at all of them, kissed the boys goodbye, and flew out of the apartment.

Alexei and Mike shared a long look. *What the hell was that?*

Alexei shrugged and went back to making breakfast.

Alexei smirked as he walked back into Rupert and Callum's apartment later that morning, amused by Oliver and Mike dashing to the tree to tuck a pile of newly-wrapped gifts among the others already stacked there. He winked at Mike over Oliver's head, then pretended to be oblivious when Oliver turned to squint up at him suspiciously.

He'd been practicing his perfectly innocent face all the way home from his shopping expedition. He and Mike would be busy that night assembling their big gift to Christian and Oliver and their fathers. Alexei was still torn about whether it was enough of a gift to give Rupert and Callum, but he was stumped on what else they could give two men who had become like brothers to them over the past year.

It was a tricky year for Christmas presents all around, for

Alexei. He was pretty sure he'd gotten the perfect gift for Mike. As certain as he felt, he still had bouts of nerves. But watching Mike run his hands through Oliver's hair and smiling at Christian, the huge tree glowing behind him, the nerves weren't anywhere to be found.

Mike came to where he hovered in the doorway still and kissed him hello. "How'd it go?"

Alexei grimaced, recalling the past two hours. "Remind me to never, ever put off shopping until Christmas Eve again. It would take an honest-to-god Christmas miracle to get me to go back into a store again today."

Mike laughed and kissed him again, perhaps thinking that would soothe Alexei's ragged nerves.

And, actually, it worked.

Alexei and Mike both cocked their heads when they felt the vibrations from the elevator through the floor. Rupert and Callum, after disappearing for several hours, were apparently home.

Alexei wondered what they could possibly have been up to. They'd answered his texts with enough vague non-answers to make Alexei suspect they had a surprise in store.

Nothing could have prepared him for what that surprise was.

Mike opened the door to the apartment when the lift came to a stop, and the boys turned to look as Rupert came through the door with a huge grin on his face, followed closely by Callum carrying a small bundle of blankets. He was grinning, too.

He stopped and then carefully turned the bundle so they could all see what was tucked inside.

A baby.

Alexei's heart stopped as tiny blue eyes stared vaguely at all of them.

Christian shot to his feet from the couch.

Oliver ran to Callum. "Who is that?"

Callum crouched down so Oliver could see the baby better,

49

and they all leaned in. Mike's hand slipped into Alexei's, and he jolted when Christian ran into him in order to peer over his shoulder. He hadn't been aware he'd stopped breathing when his eyes had locked onto that perfect little face.

"This," Callum said, putting his arm around Oliver's shoulder and pulling him closer, "is Eleanor."

Christian slid past Alexei and knelt in the middle of their little circle. Callum slipped the baby—Eleanor—into Christian's arms, careful to support her until he was certain Christian had her safely tucked close.

Christian looked down at the little girl like he'd never seen anything like her. Or anything so beautiful. "Is she ours?" he asked with wonder in his voice.

Rupert leaned against Alexei and let out a damp chuckle. Alexei immediately wrapped an arm around his shoulders.

"She's going to stay with us," Rupert explained.

"Forever?" Oliver asked, hopeful.

Callum looked up at his husband, and Alexei wasn't surprised to see Oliver wasn't the only one practically radiating hope.

"We're not sure," Rupert admitted slowly. "Eleanor's mother was staying at Pathways, but sometime last night she disappeared. Gabriel called us because we're registered foster parents, and he knows"—Rupert swallowed heavily—"that we would want to take care of her if her mother couldn't."

Christian and Oliver both nodded, as if this were obvious.

"Just like you did when my mum left me," Oliver said in a perfectly matter-of-fact voice.

Callum pulled the little boy closer. "Yeah, Ollie. Just like that."

"What if she comes back?" Oliver asked, and it was clear he was worried.

"She might," Callum admitted, "but we told Gabriel that if she did, we would welcome her here, too. Even if it's just to visit."

"Like I do with my dad now?" Christian asked. He'd seen his

father a handful of times since he'd successfully managed sobriety for six months straight. Christian had refused at first, but agreed to it after his father had signed away custody permanently to Rupert and Callum. Though he still wouldn't go without one of his new fathers, Mike, or Alexei with him.

"Maybe like that," Callum said, though it was clear he didn't really know what was going to happen. "It's a little different than with your father. Eleanor's mother is very young." He looked at Christian and frowned. "Not much older than you. She's fourteen."

"Oh, no," whispered Mike. "That's...did she have somewhere to go?"

"Gabriel is trying to figure that out. Her parents, apparently, are not an option."

For a moment no one said anything. Of the six—now seven, Alexei supposed—of them, only Callum shared a close relationship with his biological parents. The rest of them had built a family with each other. A family, it seemed, that had more than enough room in their hearts for one more.

Oliver stroked the tuft of hair on Eleanor's head, and she was so tiny that even his little hand looked large by comparison. Alexei experienced a wave of protectiveness so fierce, it felt like panic.

She was so small. So vulnerable. And all she had was them. Which, actually, was pretty fucking great. But there was work to be done.

"She needs a crib," he said, out of nowhere. Eleanor startled, her face scrunching up for a moment. Everyone seemed to hold her breath until she settled back to gazing curiously at Christian.

Callum laughed quietly. "She needs a lot more than that," he said, his voice low. He stood and went back out into the hallway, returning with a grocery sack and tattered backpack. "All we have is formula and the few things Eleanor's mother left behind."

Christian went to stand up and Rupert reached to steady him and Eleanor. When Christian looked alarmed, Alexei acted without thinking.

He plucked Eleanor from his arms and held her in his hands. Literally.

She fit into his hands. With room to spare.

Mike hooked his chin over Alexei's shoulder and ran a finger down Eleanor's cheek. "She's beautiful."

Alexei thought that if his biology had been different, he might have ovulated on the spot. The pang of longing was sharper than any he'd felt. Before, he'd known, vaguely, that he wanted to have children one day. He knew Mike did, too. Now that went from vague hope for the future to something that felt a lot more like *the plan*.

He was also never more certain that he'd got Mike the right gift for Christmas.

"We need to go shopping," Rupert said with a resigned sigh. "Can you hang around here a bit longer while we do that?"

"No," Alexei said firmly, his voice quiet. Everyone looked surprised. He huffed and tipped Eleanor up onto his shoulder. "I mean, no, Mike and I will do it. You stay here and get Eleanor as settled as you can. We'll get everything you need."

"But—"

"No, Alexei's right," Mike said quickly. "You stay here. Maybe start clearing out the office? We'll take care of the rest."

Alexei ran his hands over Eleanor's back in slow circles and thought about facing the crowds in the stores again. That wouldn't be nearly as hard as giving Eleanor to someone else to hold when it was no longer his turn.

Or not making a total fool of himself when Mike took her, and all he could do was rock on his feet and smile down at her with such absolute happiness on his face.

By the time he and Mike had assembled a list, made up a plan of action, and were ready to go, Callum and Rupert were shooting them amused and pitying looks.

Rupert plucked Eleanor from Alexei's arms. "Thank you," he said, a grin forming. "You know, Alexei, I don't think I've ever heard you speak so softly. I wasn't sure you *could*."

"Shut up," Alexei muttered, pretending to be annoyed. The fact that he said it so quietly only made Rupert grin more.

Mike laughed as he opened the door and held it. "Come on, big guy. We've got credit cards to burn."

Alexei cast one last look at Eleanor and stepped into the hallway.

"Don't go crazy, you two," Rupert called behind them. He tucked Eleanor against his chest, his cheek pressed to the top of her head. "This could only be temporary." He barely managed to choke out that reminder.

Alexei nodded and closed the door behind them.

Mike looked at the door for a long moment, then at Alexei. "That poor baby. No one should have to be without their family on Christmas."

Alexei towed Mike into a long hug. "I know, my love."

Three hours later, Mike staggered onto the elevator with the last of their purchases. He would defy anyone, *ever*, to execute a more precision shopping trip. And on Christmas Eve, no less. He and Alexei had gone to three stores and come back with the bed of Alexei's pick-up stuffed with supplies and surprises. Now it was all loaded into the lift, along with him and Alexei—who was on his phone *again.*

Mike couldn't imagine who he was texting now. It had made sense to send Rupert and Callum pictures and questions as they went through the stores, since most of these decisions really were up to them, but now they were home and going to see them in about two minutes. Couldn't whatever else Alexei wanted to tell them wait?

Mike shook his head at his boyfriend—not that Alexei noticed—and tried to decide what they would tackle first once they were unloaded. Maybe the crib. No, the bassinette. The saleswoman and Callum's mom had both assured them that for the next few weeks, at least, Eleanor would probably need to sleep in Rupert and Callum's room. It would make late-night feedings and diaper changes easier.

Maybe the changing table after that. Oh, and they had to get the tub set up and see if it would fit in the sink. And clean the bottles and—

The lift jerked to a stop and Mike heaved the doors open with a rueful smile at himself. It was going to be a busy day.

He led the way to Rupert and Callum's apartment, his attention focused on squeezing the huge bag of bedding and clothes through the door with him. It wasn't until he was standing in the foyer that he noticed the normally chaotic apartment was silent.

He looked up, alarmed, and for a moment stood silent, gaping, and wondered if he was seeing things.

"Hi, Mike," his sister Jayne said cheerfully, as if it were perfectly normal for her to be standing in the middle of Rupert and Callum's living room with Eleanor in her arms. She turned and passed the baby off to Callum, though, when it became clear Mike was having a hard time processing what he was seeing.

Mike dropped the bag he held, its contents scattering into the hallway. "What? How—you—"

He gave up trying to say anything sensible and lurched toward her. She met him halfway, both of them dancing over baby stuff to avoid stepping on it, and jumped into his arms.

Mike hugged her so tight she squeaked.

"Merry Christmas," she said, almost strangling him back.

Mike spun her around, stopping when he caught sight of Alexei hovering in the doorway, smiling fondly at them both.

"Thank you," Mike said in Russian, his voice rough. He had no doubt this had been Alexei's doing.

"You're welcome, my love," he said back.

Jayne pushed at his shoulder and he let her feet drop back onto the floor. "What are you two saying? And when did you learn Russian?" she asked, poking at Mike's stomach.

"Mike said thank you and Alexei said you're welcome and called Mike one of those gross names they call each other," Oliver supplied helpfully.

Alexei and Mike laughed. Rupert looked stunned as he stood rocking Eleanor slowly. "Wait. When did *you* learn Russian, Oliver?"

"Alexei has been teaching me and Mike. We practice together sometimes."

"Huh," Rupert said with crooked smile for Alexei. Alexei's cheeks went pink.

Mike turned back to Jayne. "I can't believe you're here. You said you had to spend Christmas in Toronto. I sent your gifts there!"

Jayne pointed under the tree. "And now they're here. Thank god you didn't send me anything really big, or I would have had to pay Air Canada for extra luggage."

"So you're staying? For Christmas?"

Jayne rolled her eyes. "Of course I am. I have to be back in three days, but you're stuck with me until then."

"Wow, that's...wow. I'm so happy to see you," Mike said fervently, hugging his sister again. They hadn't spent a holiday together in four years. In fact, they'd hardly gotten to see each other at all since he'd come out to his parents. He hadn't been home once since then.

Which reminded him. He hated to ask, but..."What about Mom and Dad?"

"What about them?"

"Didn't you want to spend Christmas with them?"

"Honestly? No. I haven't wanted to for years. I couldn't afford the flight anyway, and they didn't offer to fly me home, unlike your darling boyfriend over there."

Mike looked at Alexei again, feeling a twinge of guilt when he saw Alexei and Callum were dragging in all the boxes and bags from the elevator. "He did?"

"He gave me a choice. Here or home. I guess it's pretty obvious which I chose."

Mike left his sister and went to Alexei, pulling the bags from his hands and dropping them to the floor before he kissed him.

Alexei's arms circled him immediately.

"There are children present!" Rupert called from the kitchen, though he didn't seem particularly bothered, based on how his voice shook with laughter.

Mike drew back and smiled down at Alexei. "Thank you. Best Christmas present ever."

Alexei just rolled his eyes and chuckled.

Alexei flopped face first onto their bed at approximately ass o'clock in the morning. The mattress shook as Mike landed next to him.

"Oh my god," Mike groaned into the bedding. "I didn't think we'd ever get it all done."

Alexei would have chuckled, but he didn't have the energy left to do it. "I almost cried when Jayne went to bed," he admitted.

"You're the one that insisted we didn't need her help and that she should get some rest."

"I'm a good host."

Mike rolled his face across the comforter so that he could look at Alexei. His smile caused that chest-tightening thing in Alexei again. "You're amazing," Mike said, his voice warm. "Thank you for bringing Jayne here. And for all my other Christmas presents."

Now Alexei did chuckle, since he hadn't actually given Mike *any* of his Christmas gifts yet. Jayne coming to Christmas was as it should be, not a *gift*. It was what Mike wanted. And the whole thing with Erik had just been dumb luck, as far as timing went. It could have happened in March, if that's when they had found the time.

Rather than tell Mike any of this, Alexei just reached out and ran his hand through Mike's hair, cupping the back of his head to tug him closer.

Mike groaned with the effort, but dragged himself the last foot closer until their mouths met.

There were so many things Alexei wanted. All the time. Always. But his body just wasn't going to cooperate tonight. He hurt all over, but his knees, in particular, were going to take days to forgive him, which was *bad*. Hockey goalies' knees and hips were precious, and Alexei's didn't have a lot of mileage left in them.

Not that he regretted abusing them today. He was happy to have assembled the crib, then the bouncy seat, and the swing and the bassinette and the changing table. While he'd done that, Mike had either helped him or helped the others move the contents of the office into storage or a corner of the dining room. It was going to be cramped, but this way Rupert and Callum still had a place to work.

Jayne had spent that time opening all the other packages and separating them into piles. Then she'd gone to the store to get special laundry detergent that was safe for babies—*who knew?*—and run all the clothes and blankets through the wash.

And, of course, everyone's work took longer than it should have, because not one of them could resist taking turns holding Eleanor. They also all made a point of spending time with Oliver and Christian, neither of whom seemed any less fascinated with Eleanor than the grown-ups.

Once they'd had dinner and the kids had gone to sleep, Mike, Alexei, and Jayne had said their goodnights and gone back to their apartment. They'd hovered around the door, giggling like children, until after five minutes, Alexei had grabbed a six-pack and they'd snuck down the fire stairs to the first floor.

That's when the real work had begun.

They'd swept out a large area in the corner of the unfinished concrete floor they'd been using as garage space, then washed it thoroughly, all the while talking. Mike had put music on in his car and left the doors open so they'd have something to fill the silences, but there hadn't been any. Mike and Jayne had caught up on mutual friends and family and Alexei had listened in, happy to get to know Mike's sister better. They'd spent time together in the past, but this time felt different. Now she was on her own, no longer beholden to her parents for tuition or anything else. And the first thing she'd done was elect to spend the holidays with them. With Mike.

Alexei knew Mike missed his family in some ways, especially around the holidays, and the smile on his face, the smile *in his eyes*, made Alexei happy, too.

Once the floor had been perfectly clean, Alexei had caught Jayne yawning and sent her off to bed. Then he and Mike had crawled around with cans of paint until Alexei's back was throbbing and his knees were screaming at him to get up.

Putting up the basketball hoop to complete the half court was pretty easy after that. Even better was coming upstairs to find Jayne had finished cleaning up the pots and pans he'd left soaking from dinner with Erik the night before.

Alexei pulled back from kissing Mike. "Your sister is pretty great."

Mike made a sour face. "Can we not talk about my sister while I'm getting an erection?"

Alexei laughed and swatted Mike on the ass. "Come on, then. Get up! Let's get ready for bed."

Mike groaned but managed to lever himself off the mattress, reaching down to pull Alexei up after him. They shuffled around the room, stripping off filthy work clothes, brushing their teeth, and climbing in and out of the shower quickly, their bodies brushing here and there but both of them too tired to do anything about it.

Alexei sighed as he slipped into bed, the sheets cool and heavenly. Mike crawled in, too, and they met in the middle for a long, gentle kiss. Alexei would have sworn, ten seconds ago, that he was too tired to do anything. But then Mike wriggled closer and hummed against his lips, and Alexei's body was just *programmed* to respond.

He drew the front of Mike's boxer briefs down, tucking the waistband beneath his balls and lifting his growing erection between their bellies. Alexei wriggled his pajama pants down until his own cock was freed, and then curled his hand around both their shafts.

Mike gasped against his lips, his hips jerking in a little circle as Alexei slowly drew his hand up the length of their shafts, letting them shift and roll against one another. It should have been too dry, but Mike's skin felt like silk against his, his rigid shaft creating the perfect friction.

On his next pass, Alexei collected the precome gathering on the heads of their cocks with a swipe of his thumb. His hips worked against Mike's gently, their lips clinging and tongues tangling in a long, languid dance.

He knew when Mike was close, the motion of his hips going jerky and uncoordinated. He smiled against Mike's lips and kept up the slow pace, making them both a little crazy with its relentless rhythm. Mike's fingers dug into Alexei's biceps, his legs moving restlessly over the sheets.

Alexei kissed him harder, deeper, but his hand remained at the same maddeningly even pace. Mike whined, deep in his throat, and kissed Alexei back.

Alexei rolled over Mike, pressing Mike's back to the mattress and their hips together. A shiver worked its way down Alexei's spine, as it always did when Mike was so pliant, so easy for him. Mike was several inches taller and more than fifteen pounds heavier than Alexei, but he gave himself over without thought.

Alexei tugged harder, faster, their cocks slipping through his fist, his breath hitching against Mike's lips. He felt the heat pooling at the base of his spine, the tension drawing his balls up tight.

He planted his knees more firmly on the bed and whispered against Mike's lips.

"Come now, Michael."

Mike arched beneath him, his body even more thoroughly programmed than Alexei's, finely tuned to respond to the sound of Alexei's voice. To those words, in particular.

Mike sucked in a deep, shaky breath, and Alexei sealed Mike's lips with his own before Mike could shout and wake his sister. Mike shook, the hot pulses of his orgasm coating Alexei's fingers, slicking them both, until Alexei shuddered and let himself fall over the edge.

Alexei came back to himself some time later, slightly appalled to realize he may have passed from blissed-out-orgasm to half-asleep, lying on top of Mike with his hand trapped between their bodies. Mike gave him a sleepy smile and a gentle kiss to his lips.

"I thought I was going to have to wake you up," he teased.

Alexei grunted and dragged himself off Mike, hating to leave all that warmth. He made quick work of collecting a warm washcloth from the bathroom and cleaning them both up. The moment he slid back under the covers, Mike rolled half on top of him, his head on Alexei's shoulder, his nose tucked to Alexei's neck.

"I love you," he murmured.

"I love you, too."

"Thank you for bringing Jayne here. That really is the best Christmas present ever."

Alexei smiled and ran his hand through Mike's hair, the other trailing down Mike's back. "I thought Erik's dick was the best Christmas present ever."

Mike hummed and Alexei could feel how Mike's ass clenched just thinking about it, the muscles shifting under Alexei's palm.

Alexei chuckled.

"Shut up," Mike murmured affectionately.

Chapter Five

Mike woke with his face still plastered to Alexei's chest. He didn't think either of them had moved an inch since they'd passed out together the night before. He squinted at the light hitting his eyes, his brain too slow to realize that it was coming from the hallway until the sound of a throat being cleared reached him.

He glanced over his shoulder to find his sister standing in the doorway, a hand over her eyes. "I'm sorry to intrude," she said, smirking.

Alexei muttered in his sleep and pulled Mike closer.

Mike ran a soothing hand down Alexei's ribs. "You can open your eyes, Jayne," he said. "I mean, unless the sight of our bare, manly chests will traumatize you."

She dropped her hand, probably to be sure he could see how hard she was rolling her eyes. She did blink at Alexei's broad shoulders for a moment, though.

It was Mike's turn to smirk. "Did you need something?"

Jayne waggled her phone back and forth at him. "Have you heard your phones going off like it's...well, like it's *Christmas*?"

Mike chuckled and reached for the bedside table. Alexei's arm encircled his waist and tried to pull him back down but Mike managed to snag his cell in his fingertips. There was a series of messages, starting at six-thirty that morning, from Christian. He opened them.

Come over now?

Please?

Oliver says hurry up.

Hello??? Wake up! You can't sleep late on Christmas!!!!

WAKE UP WAKE UP WAKE UP

Ugh you guys are the worst.

Mike grinned at his phone and poked Alexei in the side. Alexei groaned and kept his eyes stubbornly shut. Mike wasn't buying it, but he let Alexei pretend.

"I'll get this big lug up. You can go over now, if you want."

Jayne just shook her head. "I'll wait. But hurry up!"

It took considerable poking and prodding to get Alexei out of bed. Mike frowned as he watched Alexei limp to the bathroom, cursing himself for letting Alexei do all that work on the basketball court. The boys were going to love it, but it wasn't worth this.

Then again, no one could have anticipated how much work they would put into getting little Eleanor settled.

Eleanor.

Mike threw on his pajamas and tossed a t-shirt for Alexei on the bed before dashing out to find his sister fidgeting by the door. She looked about as eager as he expected Oliver to be when they got across the hall. He laughed at her and pulled out all the treats they were bringing over this morning. Because, as if they hadn't been busy enough, Alexei had spent the day *before* yesterday baking until they'd had to leave for the game.

Mike was just stacking the last of the boxes when Alexei's arms curled around his waist from behind and soft lips pressed to the nape of his neck.

"Thank you, Michael," he said softly, then left him to stand there stupidly for a moment.

Michael? It was his name, of course, but reserved for special moments. Mike looked over at Alexei and blinked at the warm, happy smile he received in return.

Alexei was acting weird. Not that his boyfriend wasn't always loving and tactile, but this seemed...different. More, somehow.

Shrugging to himself, he followed Alexei and Jayne across the hall, distracted from his thoughts the moment they entered the chaos that was Rupert and Callum's home. Oliver squealed with joy to see them, *"finally"*. Mike pointed out that it was, in fact, only seven in the morning, but Oliver wasn't having it.

As far as five year olds were concerned, that was like noon when it came to Christmas.

Rupert and Callum, both of whom looked like they'd been hit by a truck, hugged them hello and tried to shoo them into the living room to get settled. Alexei ignored them, taking over the kitchen and barking out demands for requests while Jayne snuggled Eleanor and Mike got Eleanor's new fathers settled on the couch.

"Long night?" he asked with a pitying smile.

"Yes, very. We hardly slept," Callum said, rubbing his hand over his eyes. Then he looked at Rupert, and they smiled at each other like it had been the best night of their lives.

"Ugh. You guys are so gross," Christian said as he flopped down beside his dads and snuggled up under Callum's arm.

Mike secretly agreed, but he thought that kind of gross was awesome, so who was he to judge?

"Are we ready?" Oliver demanded from in front of the tree, his hands on his hips and his expression making it perfectly clear he couldn't believe how slow they were all being.

Alexei came over and passed around coffee, orange juice, and slices of coffee cake. As soon as he'd made sure everyone was going to be properly fed, he dropped onto the couch next to Mike and tugged the blanket over their legs. Mike leaned against his chest and settled in.

The Morrison family had a tradition where the youngest person present for Christmas morning had to be "the elf", so it fell to Oliver to pick out the gifts, read the tags, and hand them out, one gift to each person at a time.

He'd looked supremely scandalized that his having learned to read meant he had to *work* on Christmas morning, but then he'd learned that this also meant he got to go first, and suddenly he'd been on board with the plan.

Mike was on board with it the moment he'd realized he'd get to spend all of Christmas morning curled up on the couch with Alexei. This year it was even better, with Jayne on his other side, their shoulders bumping when they shared a joke or laughed at something the kids did. He was touched to see that Rupert and Callum and the boys had all picked out gifts for Jayne, and he could see she was, too.

"You have really nice friends," she said.

"Not friends," Mike explained. "Family."

"I hope I'm still counted among that number."

Alexei leaned over Mike. "Of course you are."

"Of course you are," Rupert repeated as he stepped over their legs en route to the coffee maker.

He and Callum really did look as though they'd pulled an all-nighter. Mike decided his and Alexei's spontaneous additional Christmas gift should be enforced naptime later. For the dads, at least, if not the kids.

As soon as it came time to open the "big presents", Mike said exactly that. Callum and Rupert looked so grateful, it was kind of pathetic. Mike was glad he and Alexei would be here to help them get used to having a newborn in the house. He looked at how Alexei smiled down at Eleanor, tucked into the crook of his elbow, and hoped that someday Rupert and Callum would be able to return the favor.

Though, Mike thought as he shifted against the couch cushions, still able to feel some of the effects of their night with Erik, maybe not right away. They still had some adventures to go on first, and were enjoying being family to *these* children now.

He snapped out of his reverie when Alexei shifted against him and stood. "Are you all ready for Mike's and my big gift?" he asked.

"You mean the naps aren't the big gift?" Callum asked.

"We have many big gifts for you this year," Alexei promised, and Mike looked at him curiously, since as far as he knew, there was only the basketball court.

Which, unsurprisingly, the boys were absolutely ecstatic over as soon as they reached the first floor.

Christian ran to the rack and grabbed a ball, then showed Oliver how to dribble while the adults looked on, clinging to their coffee mugs and smiling at the boys' excited jabbering.

"Thank you," Callum said, throwing his arm around Mike's shoulders.

"It's meant to be for all of you, but I know it's really more for the boys."

"I'll enjoy it, too," Callum promised. "When I'm not about to fall asleep on my feet."

"We have another gift for you and Rupert," Alexei said, surprising no one more than Mike. "One that I think you'll get more use out of."

Mike wondered what the heck he was talking about.

"We were going to build more apartments on the third floor," Alexei began, and Mike started to smile, immediately guessing where his brilliant boyfriend was going. "But now I think instead, we should put a staircase in your unit and build you and your growing family another floor."

"What?" Rupert asked, clearly stunned. Mike was a little alarmed to see tears forming in his wide eyes.

Jesus Christ, the poor guy clearly needed some sleep. It was a nice gift, an awesome one, even, but really.

Alexei continued quickly. "We can move your bedrooms downstairs and add a few more," he said, then eyed the boys and Eleanor. "Maybe five total?...Or *six*?" he asked when he saw how Callum smirked.

"We can convert Christian's room back into an office. And what is now Eleanor's room would be the perfect place to put the staircase," Mike said, throwing out ideas as quickly as they came to him. He stared off into the middle distance, rearranging the rooms in his head. He was already excited to get started on the project. "And you can convert the master bedroom into a guest suite, Callum, so that your parents don't have to navigate the stairs or bother with the elevator when they visit."

Alexei grinned at Mike, and Mike smiled helplessly back. Until, that is, Rupert gave out a hiccupping breath that was almost a sob.

Callum pulled Rupert in close, holding him against his chest, and smiled apologetically. "Rupert sat up half the night rocking Eleanor, worrying about what it will mean if we get to keep her." He rubbed his hand up and down Rupert's back soothingly. "He thought we'd have to move."

"Oh," Mike said, his heart dropping. "But, of course, if you want to move, we—"

"No!" Rupert's head came up and he smiled ruefully as they all got a look at his red-rimmed eyes. "No, I don't want to move. I mean, unless you move with us."

Alexei laughed. "Then, perhaps, staying here will be easier. We'll make sure you have all the room you need."

Mike shrugged. "We won't build out the second floor underneath you, either. Just in case you need bedrooms seven through ten."

Rupert actually blanched at that, but Callum just smiled. He was one of seven children, and clearly he liked that idea just fine. Before Mike could tease Rupert about it, though, Oliver managed to get a basket and Christian let out a great whoop.

While the others were distracted by the kids, Mike hugged Alexei tight and whispered, "You're brilliant."

Alexei squeezed him back. "How would you feel if we didn't build out the space below our apartment either? In case we need the space later."

Mike jerked back and looked at Alexei, his heart knocking against his ribs. "Yeah?"

"Yeah," Alexei said, his voice gruff.

Mike couldn't stop smiling. That seemed to be sufficient answer for Alexei.

Once the boys had burnt off some energy, they all trooped back upstairs to open the rest of the presents. Rupert and Callum gave the boys a trip to Disney World with their Mimi and Grandpa Morrison, which set them off cheering and jumping around again. At this rate, Mike figured, *everyone* would be napping after lunch.

At last all the gifts had been opened, and all that was left under the tree was the envelope Mike had hidden amongst the piles of boxes while Alexei had been out the night before. Oliver picked it up and held it out to Alexei.

"It's for you."

"It is?" Alexei said, taking it from Oliver and looking puzzled when he saw Mike's handwriting on the front. He looked over at Mike. "Another gift?"

It was sweet that Alexei honestly thought that all Mike had gotten him was some new socks and a nail gun. They usually did at least one bigger gift, but Mike knew Alexei would be fine if Mike didn't do anything else.

But Mike had. And he really, really hoped Alexei would be fine with that, too.

Alexei looked down at the envelope in his hand, curious, until Mike jumped to his feet and stood in front of the tree.

"Go ahead and open it," Mike said with a smile.

Alexei studied Mike's narrowed gaze, the twitch of his hands, and wondered why Mike would possibly be nervous.

More than a little curious now, Alexei tore into the envelope. At first he didn't understand what he was seeing, though he recognized the majestic building in the picture, of course. Everyone in Moscow knew the Hotel Metropol—even Alexei, who hadn't seen it in almost twenty years.

Then Alexei shuffled the papers and two plane tickets landed on top.

Alexei slowly rose to his feet, his heart lodged somewhere in his throat, stealing his voice.

Mike stepped closer, hovering in front of Alexei. "I know you've said you'd never go back, but—"

Alexei shook his head, because he couldn't believe Mike had done this. He reached out and curled his hand around Mike's arm, trying to find the right words to express everything he was feeling. Mike frowned down at the papers now clutched in

Alexei's hand.

"We don't have to go if you really don't want to, of course," Mike said quietly. "But I called the Russian consulate in Montreal, and they said there would be no issues getting a visa, even though you renounced your Russian citizenship when you became a Canadian citizen, and I know we'll have to be careful because of those awful laws, but..." Mike finally looked at Alexei. "I want to see where you grew up. I want to eat the food, and hear the music, and I want to see where you fell and scraped your knee as a kid, and go to the museums you always talk about. I want to sit in the park and play chess and hear what it sounds like to be surrounded by people speaking your language. I want to take you home."

Alexei blinked furiously against the stinging in his eyes. This man, who had barely been more than a boy when they'd first met, who had terrified him with his unique mixture of fierce independence and a soul-deep need for submission, had become everything.

"*You* are my home, Michael," Alexei said, his voice gruff. "But I will show you all those places. I want you to see them, too."

Mike blinked, a smile blooming on his face. "So this is okay?"

"Of course it's okay," Alexei said, giving in and kissing Mike softly. "This is the best Christmas present ever."

Mike laughed, but it was kind of damp. Alexei pulled him in close, holding him tightly enough that it was difficult for either of them to breathe.

What the hell had he ever done to deserve this man?

Alexei had no idea. But he did know, he never, ever, wanted to lose him. And there was no way in hell he was waiting for the New Year to make sure Mike knew it.

"Michael, I still have one more gift to give you, too."

"You do?" Mike asked, clearly surprised but pleased.

Mike's smile fell, replaced by wide-eyed shock, when Alexei dropped to one knee before him. Alexei passed the paperwork he still clutched over to Oliver, then tucked his hand into his pocket, taking one of Mike's hands in his other.

"Michael, until I met you, I thought I knew what love was, but I was wrong. You are my heart, my best friend, my partner in business and in life. There is no one I would rather spend my life with, play hockey with, argue with, or grow old with."

He pulled his hand from his pocket and presented the two rings threaded over his index finger. Mike reached out with a shaking hand to brush his finger over them both, tears rolling down his cheeks.

"Will you do me the honor of being my husband?" Alexei asked, his voice little more than a scratch.

"Oh my god, *yes*."

Everyone whooped, but Alexei could look only at Mike as he slowly rose to his feet. Mike grabbed his elbows and steadied him when his hips and knees protested, a grin on his face. As soon as Alexei was stable, Mike took the rings and slid one onto Alexei's finger, then the other onto his own.

Alexei kissed him, once, fiercely, then gathered him into a hug. Mike buried his face against Alexei's neck and clung, and Alexei could feel how he shook, felt the tears on his neck.

A moment before their family piled on top of them, he pressed his lips to Mike's ear and whispered, "And you thought I gave you *Erik's dick* for Christmas."

Mike's snort was muffled by Alexei's shoulder and then they were both laughing, perhaps a little hysterically, as they accepted hugs and kisses and congratulations from the people they loved most.

About the Author

Samantha Wayland has three great loves in life; her family, writing books, and hockey. She is often found apologizing to the first for how much time and attention is taken up by the latter two, but they forgive her because they are awesome and she clearly doesn't deserve them.

Sam lives with her family—of both the two and four-legged variety—outside of Boston. She is a wicked passionate New Englander (born and raised) who has been known to wax rhapsodic about the Maine Coast, the mountains of New Hampshire and Vermont, and the sensible way in which her local brethren don't see a need for directional signals (blinkahs!). When she's not locked away in her home office, she can generally be found tucked in the corner of the local Thai place with other socially-starved authors and an adult beverage.

Her favorite things include mango martinis, tiny Chihuahuas with big attitude problems, and the Oxford comma.

Sam loves to hear from readers. Email her at samantha@samanthawayland.com or find her on Facebook or Twitter (@samwayland).

Also By Samantha Wayland

Crashing the Net

They never see it coming...

Mike comes to Moncton wanting nothing more than to play for the Ice Cats and finally live on his own terms. He's broke, bruised, and covered from head to toe in cheap lube, but he isn't going to let that stop him. All he needs is a place to live and some time to figure out how to reconcile who he really is with who everyone wants him to be.

Dumping three gallons of lube on the new kid is just another day at the office for Alexei. He knows exactly who he is: a goalie on the ice, a prankster in the locker room, and a man who knows better than to share his private life with anyone. He's let people in before and it's taught him that if he can't have what he really wants, it's better to be alone.

Despite their apparent differences, an unlikely friendship grows. Neither of them could ever have guessed how much they really have in common.

Changing The Rules

Their own way... their own time... their own rules...

Alexei has a roommate and it's not Mike. He also has a whole lot of regrets, but no one wanted the Ice Cats' brand new back-up goalie to be on his own down the stretch in the playoffs. Anyway, Alexei and Mike have been together a long time. They're getting married for heaven's sake. They can go a few nights not sleeping next to each other.

Mike can't stand not sleeping next to Alexei. He's not going to complain, because this is the playoffs and he's a freaking adult, but it turns out sleep deprivation makes him overthink a bunch of shit he wasn't planning to think about at all until the off-season. Like, the fact they've been engaged for over a year and haven't set a date.

Mike knows they're going to spend their lives together. But to get the wedding done? They're going to have to change some rules...

Home & Away

You can build a team, but you have to find your home.

Rupert Smythe is fond of many things. Callum Morrison isn't one of them.

Rupert is a quiet, thoughtful business man and, sadly, a total wimp. Maybe not the ideal candidate to run a professional hockey team, but he signed on to do it anyway. As his life has reminded him on an almost daily basis since, this isn't the most brilliant idea he's ever had. And that was before Callum showed up.

Being in the spotlight is just part of being a professional athlete, but Callum needs a break. He arrives in Moncton unannounced, determined to help grow the team he just bought, and under the assumption he'd be welcome. Possibly he should have tried to make a better first impression.

Callum figures he can push through the rest of the summer, never expecting two kids, a host of friends, and his growing feelings for Rupert to derail everything he has ever believed about what he wanted, and what he could have.

Checking It Twice